THE
TWIDDLE TWINS'
HAUNTED
HOUSE

THE TWIDDLE TWINS' HAUNTED HOUSE

by HOWARD GOLDSMITH

with original illustrations by

JACK KENT

Dedicated with love to Frona—H.G.

Acknowledgment
The author and publisher would like to thank June Kent for
permission to use the original art in this edition of the book.
The original art is held in the Kerlan Collection, University of
Minnesota, Minneapolis, Minnesota.

Text copyright © 1997, 1985 by Howard Goldsmith
Illustrations copyright © 1985 by Jack Kent
Hardcover edition published in 1985 by Caedmon

Designed by Christy Hale
Production by Our House

Printed in United States of America
            00 01   9 8 7 6 5 4

Library of Congress Cataloging-in-Publication data
Goldsmith, Howard.
    The Twiddle twins' haunted house / by Howard Goldsmith ; with
original illustrations by Jack Kent.
        p.   cm.
    Summary: After moving into their new house, the twins and
their parents are awakened in the middle of the night by a
strange tapping noise and are convinced that they have a ghost.
    ISBN 1-57255-222-0 (pbk.)
    [1. Moving, Household—Fiction.   2. Ghosts—Fiction.
3. Twins—Fiction.   4. Hippopotamus—Fiction.]
I. Kent, Jack, 1920- ill.   II. Title.
PZ7.G575Tw   1996
[E]—dc20   96-15258
                                               CIP
                                               AC

Contents

Who Is Knocking at the Door?

TAP. TAP. TAP.

Tabitha Twiddle opened her eyes. The tapping had woken her. She felt sleepy.

She looked at the clock. It said five o'clock. Tabitha pulled the blanket over her head. She tried to go back to sleep.

But the noise came again.

TAP. TAP. TAP.

Someone must be knocking at the door.

It was too early for visitors.

Who was at the door?

TAP. TAP. TAP.

Tabitha hopped out of bed. She went into the hall. Listening at her parents' door, she heard:

Zzzzzzzzzzz.

Mr. Twiddle was snoring. Tabitha's mother must be asleep, too. Tabitha didn't want to wake them. She decided to go downstairs and see who was there.

As Tabitha started down the steps, her twin brother Timothy opened his door. His left eye was closed.

He's still half asleep, Tabitha thought.

"Who's knocking at the door?" Timothy asked.

"I don't know. Let's go see together," said
Tabitha.

Tabitha and Timothy went downstairs.
"Who's there?" they called.

There was no answer.

They looked out the window. They didn't see anyone.

Tabitha opened the door. No one was there.

"Whoever it was went away," said Timothy.

As they started upstairs, the tapping began again. They dashed to the door. But no one was there!

"Maybe it's a ghost," said Tabitha
with a shiver.

The Twiddle
family had just
moved into this
house. Neighbors
said the house was
haunted. They heard strange
noises at night. But Mr. Twiddle didn't
believe in ghosts.

"Who's making that noise?" he asked
from the top of the stairs.

Mrs. Twiddle stood beside him, her hair in curlers.

"Someone's knocking at the door," said Tabitha.

"Who is it?" Mrs. Twiddle asked.

"No one," Timothy answered.

"WHAT?" Mr. Twiddle cried. "No one's knocking at the door?"

TAP. TAP. TAP.

"Do you call that no one?" Mr. Twiddle asked.

The Twiddles exchanged puzzled looks.

Is It a Ghost?

"The knocking is at the *back* door," said Mrs. Twiddle.

The Twiddles raced to the back of the house. Mr. Twiddle opened the door.

But no one was there.

TAP. TAP. TAP.

"It's in the next room," said Mrs. Twiddle.

They ran into the dining room. There was a tapping at the window. Mr. Twiddle pulled back the curtain.

No one was there.

No one, but some *thing*. A branch was scraping against the window.

RAP-TAP. RAP-TAP.

"There's your ghost," said Timothy. "A branch!"

"I'll take care of that," said Mr. Twiddle.

He went outside and sawed off the branch.

"Now it's quiet. We can all go back to bed," he said.

TAP. TAP. TAP.

"The ghost is back," said Tabitha.

They looked in every room, downstairs and upstairs.

"Maybe someone is throwing pebbles at the house," said Mrs. Twiddle.

Tabitha looked out the window. "I don't see anyone," she said.

Timothy ran to the front of the house. "I don't see anyone on this side either," he called.

TAP. TAP. TAP. The tapping continued.

"I knew it," said Tabitha. "It must be ghosts. The house is full of them."

"Nonsense," said Mr. Twiddle. "There is no such thing as a ghost. The plumbing must be making the noise. I'll call the plumber. He'll fix it."

Mr. Twiddle phoned the plumber. "I'll be right over," said the plumber.

The plumber looked in the basement. "The pipes are fine," he said. "Nothing's wrong down here. I don't hear any noise."

Then all of a sudden:
TAP. TAP. TAP.
The sound seemed to be everywhere
and nowhere.

"Let me out of here!" the plumber cried.
"The place is haunted!"
He flew up the stairs and out the door.
"Good-bye," called the Twiddles, waving.

The Mouse Catcher

"The tapping must be mice," Mr. Twiddle decided.

"Mice!" cried Mrs. Twiddle. Her hair curlers popped off her head.

"Don't be afraid," said Mr. Twiddle. "I'll call the mouse catcher. He'll get rid of the mice."

But the mouse catcher didn't find a single mouse hole. "I'm sure there aren't any mice in this house," he said.

Then the tapping began again. The mouse catcher said, "I have to go." He left the house as quickly as the plumber had.

"Maybe someone is tapping out a secret message," said Timothy.

"It could be the ghost of poor Aunt Tillie," said Mrs. Twiddle. "She used to tap with her cane."

Timothy and Tabitha took out their code book. Then they heard:

RAP-TAP.

RAP-TAP-TAP.

TAP-RAP. RAP-TAP.

Timothy looked through the code book. "That means 'Pass the spaghetti.' What kind of message is that?" he asked.

"It must be a hungry ghost," said
Tabitha.

Timothy's ears stood up. "Listen," he
said. "It's coming from the basement
again."

"Let's go!" said Tabitha.

The twins crept down the stairs.

TAP. TAP. TAP.

"Do you hear that?" Timothy asked. "It's getting louder."

"Those are my knees knocking together," said Tabitha. "My legs are shaking."

They entered the basement. It was dark and cool. Timothy turned on the light. The basement was empty.

They heard a tapping on the far wall. They followed the noise across the basement to the wall.

"It's coming from *outside* the house," Tabitha whispered.

"I think it *is* coming from outside," said Timothy. "Let's go see."

The Uninvited Guest

Timothy and Tabitha went out the back door into the yard.

"I don't see anyone here," said Timothy.

TAP. TAP. TAP.

It was getting louder and louder.

"What can it be?" Tabitha asked.

They crossed the yard to the other side of the house.

"Look!" Tabitha cried. "Inside the drainpipe."

Timothy's eyes popped. A bird's tail was sticking out of the drainpipe. Timothy bent down close to the ground. He looked inside the drainpipe.

"It's a woodpecker!" he cried. "It's stuck inside. It can't get out."

"Let's go call Daddy," Tabitha said. "He'll get it out."

They raced
into the house.
Mr. and Mrs. Twiddle
were sitting in the living room.

"Daddy, come quickly!" Tabitha yelled.

"What's the matter?" Mr. Twiddle asked,
jumping out of his chair.

"We found the ghost!" Timothy cried.

"A ghost!" said Mrs. Twiddle. "Let's leave this house at once."

"I was only joking," said Timothy. "The ghost is just a woodpecker."

They ran outside.

Mr. Twiddle put on a glove he used for gardening. He reached into the drainpipe and pulled out the bird.

"Poor woodpecker," said Mrs. Twiddle.
"I hope it's not hurt."

"Maybe it would like some spaghetti,"
said Tabitha.

But the woodpecker had other ideas. It
flapped its wings and flew away.

"That silly bird mistook the drainpipe for a tree trunk," said Timothy. "A hollow one."

"Speaking of hollow, my stomach feels empty," said Mr. Twiddle.

"Mine, too," said Tabitha.

"But it's too early for breakfast, isn't it?" asked Timothy.

"It's never too early for spaghetti,"
said Mrs. Twiddle. And she was right.